Also from The (

GYRFAL(

an award-winning novel for ages 9+
from Grace Wells

'Magical and marvellous first novel'
The Sunday Independent

'A very imaginative coming-of-age story ... *Gyrfalcon* will stir
the imagination of its young readers'
Leinster Leader

'Uplifting ... Seldom have I read such vivid and passionate
descriptions of the environment'
Books Ireland

'Wells has given us a striking début novel'
Robert Dunbar, The Irish Times

'A beautiful story ... I had tears in my eyes
reading this very soulful story'
Catherine Ann Cullen, The Pat Kenny Show

Award-winning poet and author Grace Wells grew up in London, England. From the earliest age her dream was to be a writer. Before being able to make that dream come true she had careers as a florist, a television producer and in arts administration. Now she lives with her partner and her two children in County Tipperary, writing and growing organic food. A full-time eco-worrier and part-time eco-warrior, she is committed to environmental protection. She likes to visit schools to discuss her work and talk with children about their heroes, heroines and dreams.

ICE DREAMS

Grace Wells

Illustrated by Lisa Jackson

THE O'BRIEN PRESS
DUBLIN

First published 2008 by The O'Brien Press Ltd,
12 Terenure Road East, Dublin 6, Ireland.
Tel: +353 1 4923333; Fax: +353 1 4922777
E-mail: books@obrien.ie
Website: www.obrien.ie

ISBN: 978-1-84717-045-3

British Library Cataloguing-in-Publication Data
Wells, Grace
Ice dreams
1. Villages - Greece - Juvenile fiction
2. Children's stories
I. Title
823.9'2[J]

1 2 3 4 5 6 7 8 9
08 09 10 11 12

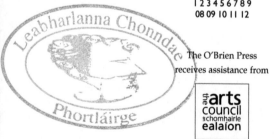

The O'Brien Press
receives assistance from

the arts
council
schomhairle
ealaíon

Layout and design: The O'Brien Press Ltd
Illustrations: Lisa Jackson
Printing: Cox and Wyman Ltd

CONTENTS

For Noah, and local things

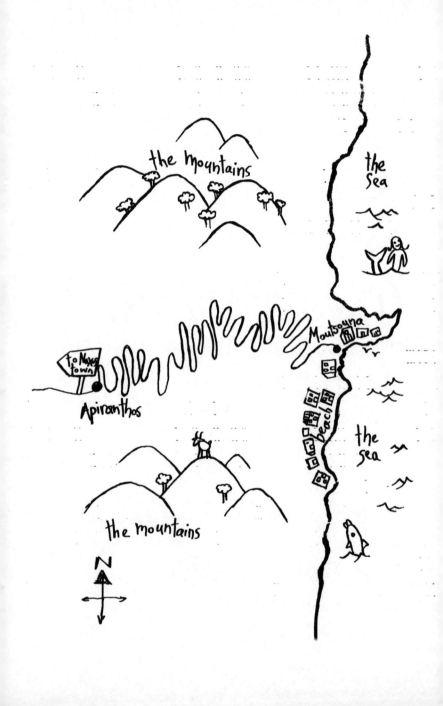

1

Meet the Family

'm going to begin by introducing everybody,' Nina said to her brother Alex.

'Mm,' Alex mumbled, as he flipped over in his bed like a pancake tossed in Mama's hot oil. He was ready and eager for sleep, and he twisted impatiently while he waited for his dreams to come.

Nina narrowed her large brown eyes. 'You're not listening to me, are you?' she asked.

Alex turned himself over to face Nina and his bright eyes swept across her face like the strong beam of the lighthouse on the headland across the bay.

'Who are you introducing?'

'Everybody,' Nina sighed. 'I've been telling you

and you haven't been listening. I've decided not to wait until I'm older to become a writer. I'm going to start my first book now, and I'm going to begin by introducing everybody.'

'Everybody?' Alex whistled, sitting up in bed. 'You can't introduce everybody in Moutsouna. It would take up a whole book to introduce everybody in the village!'

At once his inventive mind started sparking about a book that could introduce everybody in their village. He frowned. It might be a good idea. It could have an alphabetical list of all the villagers, with a picture of each person standing in front of their home. That way you would know whether they lived in one of the tall, white houses that squeezed together around the ice-factory in the harbour, or if, like he and Nina, they lived in one of the bungalows on the edge of the beach.

'Yes!' Alex nodded happily. 'It could be a special sort of village directory. Your book could list the names of a person's children and say how many goats and chickens each family had. People could look at it and see straight away how many villagers worked in the factory and how many still fished and owned boats, though that wouldn't be very many now, would it?'

'No, Alex, that isn't what I mean at all,' Nina said, rolling over to face her brother. 'This book is just about us. Our family. I'm going to begin by introducing everybody in this house.' She went on. 'I'll say, "This is Alex Papadopolos and this is Nina Papadopolos. They are twins."

Underneath, I'll have a picture of you on your bicycle with the pull-along-cart that you made, and under the picture it will say, "Alex is always inventing things."'

Alex is always inventing things.

'Mm.' Alex frowned, 'Go on. What does the picture of you show?'

'I'm not sure,' Nina sighed.

'You could draw a picture of you helping Mama make ice cream. You like doing that,' he added.

'I was going to have a picture of me writing my book. I would look very serious and hard working. I suppose the ice-cream picture might be better. It could be fun to draw all the egg shells and the jugs of cream,' Nina said thoughtfully. 'Then I need a

Nina was writing a book ...

Grandfather was the oldest man in the village. He was blind.

picture of Grandfather. I'll say that he is the oldest man in the village.'

'You had better say he has gone blind now. I don't think people could tell just from a picture,' Alex added.

'All right.' Nina nodded. 'And lastly, there'll be a

Mama Papadopolos and Papa Papadopolos.

picture of Mama and Papa. I'll label them Mama Papadopolos and Papa Papadopolos.'

'Wouldn't you just call them Eleni and Nikos?' Alex asked, pulling the white bedsheet up around his dark head.

'No,' Nina said. 'If you put too many names in a

book all at once, people get confused. Maybe later on, I might refer to Mama as Eleni, but at the beginning I'll just have the picture, and underneath it will say, "Mama Papadopolos is the school teacher in the neighbouring town of Apiranthos."'

'In the neighbouring town of Apiranthos?' Alex yawned. 'This book sounds like a guide for tourists. You'll be having a map next.'

'It is not a guidebook! It's a story about you and me, Mama, Papa and Grandfather, and how we all live together in this little house, with the goats and the chickens and the melon patch, and the lemon tree and the olive grove, and how Mama is the school teacher and Papa works in the ice-factory,' Nina said, crossly. 'And maybe, just maybe I'll put in your friend, Ios next-door, and his goat, Kalimara, and maybe I'll say his is the most stubborn goat in the whole of Greece.'

Alex frowned. He wasn't sure if anybody would want to read about stubborn goats.

Then drawing a huge breath, Nina went on, 'And

there is going to be a map so people can see we live on an island, in a small village, between the mountains and the sea. With a map it will be obvious that the only way here is by boat, or down the hairpin road. Things have to be obvious in books, because people don't like too much explanation. Explanation is boring and this isn't going to be a boring book.' Nina finished huffily, rolling over to face the wall. She closed her eyes, feeling cross and sad, thinking Alex thought her book was a bad idea.

Actually Alex did not think the book was a bad idea. He felt excited about it and, like Nina, he lay there, listening to the lap of the sea as the waves came in across the beach and, like Nina, he was imagining a map of their island, thinking of all the tiny details he would have to put on it. For he had decided he had better be the one to draw it. The map would need to be very accurate, so that people wouldn't get lost in the mountains. It would need to be very exact so readers could tell just by looking at it how very dangerous the hairpin-bend road was.

Nina twirled one lock of her brown hair around a sleepy finger. Her great long eyelashes flapped slowly at her eyes like butterflies folding their wings.

'Nina,' Alex whispered, 'I'll help you with your map. On our way to school tomorrow, we'll count the number of bends there are on the hairpin road.'

But Nina didn't answer. She was already fast asleep.

2

Bus Drivers and Hairpin Bends

Nina and Alex ran excitedly to breakfast. Thoughts of their map filled their heads and their eyes shone.

'Ha!' Papa Papadopolos said as they came to the table. 'Just by looking at you I can tell what day of the week it is! You know why?' he asked, offering Nina a slice of thick bread. Nina smiled back at him. She loved her papa. She knew what he was about to say because every Monday morning he said the same thing.

'Just by looking at your faces I can tell it's Monday or

Wednesday or Friday. You know why, eh?' Papa joked.

'Bus drivers,' Nina and Alex answered together.

'Exactly!' Papa laughed. 'Bus drivers. The clock of this whole village ticks on bus drivers.' He slapped his hand cheerfully on the table. 'Right now in every house the children are smiling.' (He smiled a big smile.) 'They're gulping their food.' (Papa gulped and chewed dramatically.) 'They're rushing their dressing. They're brushing their hair with toothbrushes they're in such a hurry.' (Papa held his fork in front of his mouth and then swept it backwards through his hair.) 'You know why?' Papa smiled, opening his arms in a big shrug.

Nina and Alex nodded, but they didn't interrupt. They liked it when Papa carried on like this.

'The whole happiness of our village depends on bus drivers. On Tuesdays and Thursdays the children wake up and sigh.' (He groaned horribly.) 'The children are miserable; they make everyone around them miserable! Why? Old Dimitri from the neighbouring town of Apiranthos!' He shook his head. 'Grumpy Dimitri. Smelly Dimitri.' He sniffed and gagged and pretended to choke.

The twins giggled.

'Oh Papa!' Mama Papadopolos frowned. 'You shouldn't say such things in front of the children. He doesn't smell. He uses aftershave, that's all.'

'Smelly Dimitri Simitas from Apiranthos! What do we say eh, my children? We say "Boo! Boo!"'

'Boo!' The children echoed, laughing.

'On Tuesdays and Thursdays, Smelly Dimitri drives the bus,' Papa went on. 'He wears mirrored sunglasses so you can't see his eyes.' (Papa put his hands in front of his face.) 'And he speaks to the children with a sharp tongue that if … if you could see it, if he let it out of his head, you would know it was forked like a snake's. Sssss!' Papa hissed.

'Oh Papa!' Mama said crossly. 'What have you got against the man?'

'It's not me; it's the children that don't like him,' Papa carried on.

'Just because he's a bit sharp with them? The bus is always on time on his days. He always drives at a nice, steady pace.'

'That's right.' Papa nodded. 'And you can drive through life in exactly the same way. You can take it very seriously, set your heart on your destination and then get impatient when anything gets in the way. Am I right, Grandfather?' Papa asked, leaning over toward his father-in-law.

Grandfather nodded slowly.

'Or,' Papa said suddenly, becoming quite calm and still, 'you can do the opposite and be like Filipos.'

The children smiled. Easily they could imagine Filipos Velcanos who drove the bus on Monday, Wednesday and Friday. Alex even imagined the tall, thin house Filipos lived in beside the ice-factory. Nina pictured his face and remembered he never wore sunglasses so you always saw his bright eyes.

'Filipos drives the bus,' Papa said, putting his arms out and steering an imaginary wheel, 'with the radio turned up loud. When his favourite songs come on he turns the volume even higher and sings along. Now Smelly Dimitri, he uses the horn when he is impatient and angry, but Filipos thinks of the horn as a musical instrument he just happens to be playing while driving a bus. At every bend in the road he gives two long blasts and shouts out Moutsouna or Apiranthos or wherever it is he's stopping next.'

'That way a person can get a headache,' Mama sighed, getting up to gather her bags.

'But no one ever has to worry they're on the wrong bus!' Papa laughed. 'And why, if you told Filipos you had a headache, he'd drive you all the way to the chemist in Naxos Town! Filipos has time for everyone, time for the tired old school mistresses with their headaches and time for small children who run and trip and drop their sticky sweets.' (He said reaching forward to put small, rustling packages in Nina and Alex's pockets.) 'Filipos drives with his heart in his hand like a handkerchief, ever ready to hand it out to whoever needs it,' Papa said. 'With Filipos the whole drive is a carnival; with him it's the journey that matters; it's how you get there, not where you're going. We never really know where we're going, do we, Grandfather?' Papa Papadopolos shrugged and the old man nodded slowly. 'And we never know what we'll meet on the way. Maybe they'll be stray goats or a stubborn donkey, or a woman with more parcels than she can carry, or a tourist who has broken down. You can beep your horn impatiently at them like Smelly Dimitri.' (Papa tooted loudly.) 'Or you can welcome them into your journey with a smile!'

Alex nodded. Filipos always welcomed everything with a smile. He welcomed the stray goats and the tourists driving down the centre of the road trying to steer away from the dangerous cliffs. Alex smiled to himself, yes, Filipos welcomed the dangerous road. He welcomed the way it had no wall to protect you. He lived his days with the back of the bus or the front of the bus hung in some precarious way over the edge of a cliff, but he always kept the four wheels squarely on the road. Driving the bus in those mountains was wild and dangerous, but Alex knew if you asked his friends what they wanted to be when they grew up and left school, all of them, girls and boys, dreamed of becoming bus drivers like Filipos.

'Come on,' Nina said suddenly to Alex, seeing Mama was ready by the door. 'We'd better get counting.'

'Counting?' Papa asked.

'Secret,' Nina said, grabbing Alex's arm and pulling him from the house. They overtook Mama as she was saying her goodbyes and ran along the dusty road until they reached the square by the harbour where the old bus waited. Its door hung open and there was Filipos smiling at them. Yes! Nina and Alex thought gladly, knowing no hairpin bend was going to slip by unnoticed while they had Filipos there hooting his horn and shouting 'Apiranthos, Apiranthos!' at each and every one.

3

Nina Needs a Story

That evening, just as every evening, the village children played football on the beach. Their parents and uncles and aunts gathered on the Papadopolos porch to watch as the last rays of the setting sun slipped behind the mountains. But Alex and Nina didn't join them; they were busy inside. As he worked, Alex could hear the adults' talk drift in through the open window. He could even hear the thud and lift of the ball, but he wasn't interested in playing right now. It was more important to finish his map.

Nina went to the window to look out. The village

was filling with purple dusk and the great blue night coming down from the hills. Across the bay the island of Dhenousa had disappeared into the dark. The swirling beam of the lighthouse on the headland flashed into the black sky.

Alex put the final details on his map. Proudly he handed it to Nina. The hairpin road had exactly thirty-six bad bends.

'Thanks, thanks so much,' Nina said, snaking her finger down the curved road. Then she folded the map carefully into the front of her new notebook.

'Alex?' she asked quietly. 'Alex, I'm worried about my book.'

'What sort of worried?' Alex smiled.

'Well in chapter one I've introduced everybody and I've drawn pictures. It's a good start, but I don't know what to put in next. What I really want is to write a book that children say is their favourite book ever.'

'You could never write a book as good as that!'

Alex pouted. 'Most favourite books have already been written.'

That made Nina cross. 'That's like saying all the best inventions have already been invented. If I said that, would you stop inventing things?'

Alex looked at her very seriously. He had to admit Nina had a point. Even if he thought all the best inventions had already been invented, it would never stop him from trying to invent more.

'Of course not.' Alex nodded. He thought for a moment. 'A favourite book has to be about something children love. Like sweets,' Alex said.

'I don't want to write about sweets,' Nina moaned.

'Or about a person that children love. Like Santa Claus,' Alex suggested.

'I don't want to write about Santa Claus,' Nina sighed. 'I want to write about us.'

'You could put in some of my inventions if you like,' Alex offered.

Nina frowned.

'You could put in my car-that-steers-by-itself or my bicycle-that-powers-uphill? I've drawings of my kite-that-doesn't-get-stuck-in-olive-trees, but I'm still working on my plane-that-doesn't-break-when-it-crashes. You could have that when I'm ready?'

'That's kind of you Alex, but you know, what I really need is a story.'

'A story?' Alex puzzled.

'Yes, a story about all these people that live in this house.'

'Well if you want a story, you should be out on the porch with the adults. You should be sitting listening to Grandfather,' Alex said.

'Of course! That's what I need, one of Grandfather's stories!' Nina smiled at him and then turned on her heels and ran, notebook in hand, out of the room. Alex followed after her.

Outside aunts and uncles and children had settled like roosting birds. In his rocking chair in the centre of the porch sat Grandfather. The smaller children crept to sit close by. Like their older brothers and sisters they were a little bit frightened of him. It was whispered that his blindness gave him special powers. It was said he could see things that no one else could and he could smell things before they ever happened. The children were afraid he could read their minds. Yet, despite their fear, they drew around as if he were a fire that kept them warm. For Grandfather was the oldest person in their village and as Mama Papadopolos always said, he was a living book, a history book of Moutsouna, that someone had better write down.

Nina went to sit on Mama's lap. Alex came out to find Papa's knee. His big arms wrapped Alex in a tight hug and Alex could smell that fresh icy scent that all the men who worked in the factory came home with.

Suddenly the boy next door, Ios, got up and went shyly to the grandfather.

'Will you tell a story about my people, please?' he asked.

The grandfather's worn hands lifted slowly to Ios' face. Gently, the old man felt the boy's forehead; his fingers sketched around his eyes and then back to feel Ios' ears. They stuck out strongly from the sides of his head.

The children watched transfixed. Often they copied him, running wild and blindfold in the olive groves. They tried to guess one another by their ears or noses, but no one could do it like the grandfather.

'Ah, it is Ios,' Grandfather said. 'You have your mother's eyes and your father's forehead, but those ears, those ears go back a long way in time. Those ears belong to the goat-herders of the Gap of the Winds.'

A sudden hush came over the adults.

'The goat-herders of the Gap of the Winds,' Grandfather repeated, shaking his head sadly.

Ios shook a little and the small children's eyes grew round.

'Boy,' Grandfather said, grabbing Ios by the arm,

'are you brave enough to hear what happened to the goat-herders of the Gap of the Winds?'

'Yes,' Ios whispered and a little thrill of terror went around the porch.

4

The Goat-herders of the Gap of the Winds

'When I was a child,' Grandfather began, 'we gathered here in the evenings, just as we all are now, but back then we watched candles and oil lights flickering in the windows. There were more windows then. Across the bay.' He pointed above the children's heads out towards Dhenousa. 'There were lights on that island once. And up there, behind us, in the mountains were the little lights of the Windmill village, where the flour was milled. To the south were the lights of Falifico, where they made the pots and jugs and so on. All gone,' he said in a deep voice that stilled the sounds of the night. Even the small waves lapping on the beach and the crickets busy in the ditches seemed to hush at the grandfather's words.

'Up there, right between the two high peaks is the valley known as the Gap of the Winds. You wouldn't even know it was there now, would you?' the grandfather asked, staring in the direction of the black mountains.

'There must have been nine or ten goat-herding families living there once upon a time. They were famous people, hardy and strong, and you knew them by their ears, for it was said that the wind always blew through that valley, and with it blew the secrets of Moutsouna and Apiranthos, Falifico and Naxos Town, even the secrets of Athens itself. And anybody's ears would stick out if they had to listen to the secrets of a whole city.'

The grandfather fell silent. At last he whispered,

'All gone. Changes came. Progress. Progress suddenly brought factories. Everything we islanders had done by hand for hundreds of years was now being done by machines. All over the mainland, factories were spitting out pots and flour and clothes and cheese made by machines.'

He paused for a moment to allow the children think what this might mean.

'In the beginning all those machine-made things could be bought quite cheaply. And buy them the people did. For who would want to spend days carrying water to grow wheat, and spend hours milling it, when you could buy a packet of flour in the shop? Who wanted to sit for a week weaving and sewing, when you could buy some ready-made clothes? Who, in their right mind, would chase goats over mountains, or spend days making a good cheese, when you could eat a bad one from a packet?'

'The old ways were cast aside. Before you could swap cheese and butter with your neighbour for flour or eggs, but now everybody wanted money.

Before, people had grown what they ate. They'd made what they needed. Not any more. And the fact was they had no money in the islands. To get money our people sold things. First they sold their grandmother's lace or the furniture their fathers had made. But when that was all gone they started to sell their land and their homes and they began to move away to Naxos Town, or to Athens itself.'

The children were silent. They knew these stories; all their lives they had heard such things. Even the smallest of them had ideas of how the islands had once been full of people who had all had to move away.

'The goat-herders of the Gap of the Winds were hit the hardest of all, for their land was too high up and too windy, and the people had got too lazy for that kind of land. No one would buy it. In the end the goat-herders had to leave with nothing. They walked to Naxos Town with only the clothes on their backs and their memories in their hearts. They stowed themselves away on a ferry to Athens. But they had no money and a city is never kind to a person with no money. Athens chewed up the goat-herders of the Gap of the Winds. It chewed them up and spat them out and left them begging on the streets, and I fear Ios, you are all that is left of them.'

'And how is it that I am left at all?' Ios asked.

'Only this,' Grandfather answered. 'Only that, long ago, your great-grandmother came down from the Gap to barter cheese every week. In that way, she met your great-grandfather. In time, she married him and came to live here in the village and that saved her, for the rest of them are gone.'

Grandfather paused; the words seemed to hover around his lips, but his voice was gone. Then quietly, in a whisper, he said, 'drop by drop, one by one, through my life I've seen the people leave. I've seen the lights of the island extinguished. And with every light go the goats and the melons and the children. And when the children go, the future of a place goes and there is nothing left.' The grandfather finished sorrowfully and the waves that rolled up onto the shore echoed with a soft sound like crying.

Alex jumped up from Papa's lap. He stepped across the dark porch to reach his grandfather's hand. 'We're still here, Grandfather. The lights of Moutsouna will never go out,' he said bravely.

'It's only the ice-factory that keeps us here,' the grandfather said sadly. 'If anything happens to that factory we'll be on the first ferry to Athens.'

The adults all sighed. Mama Papadopolos looked over their troubled faces. She knew Grandfather was right; the village depended on that factory. Even though she had her job as a teacher, it only existed as long as there were children to teach. She knew if there were no Moutsouna children, the school in Apiranthos would have to close. Then the Apiranthos children would have to take buses all the way across the island to Naxos Town to go to school. But nobody wanted their children to sit on buses for four hours a day! Before long, Apiranthos would be in danger too.

'Enough!' Papa Papadopolos suddenly roared, and they all nearly jumped out of their skins with fright as he stood up and waved clenched fists in the air.

'Enough!' he roared. 'All my life I have heard these stories. Athens! Athens! Athens! That's all I ever hear. No more now! We are never going to leave Moutsouna. My people have lived here for hundreds of years. They will carry on living here for hundreds of years!' He slammed his fist down on the table, and in one movement all the visiting children jumped up and ran away into the night screaming.

Papa glowered in the darkness. 'They'll be no more talk of Athens. If anybody ... anybody ever mentions Athens ... I'll ... I'll ...'

'Bedtime!' Mama said quickly, her eyes wide and definite.

The adults nodded and began to leave their seats. Nina and Alex stood up and went into the house. They were used to their Papa shouting about things from time to time, but tonight he had been at his most dramatic. They cleaned their teeth and got into bed, but every time they thought of the moment when Papa Papadopolos had slammed his fist on the table, making the children run off into the night, it made them laugh. They lay in their beds trying to be quiet, but they were too excited to sleep. After a while, Alex whispered, 'what's the capital city of France, Nina?'

'Paris,' she whispered.

'The capital city of England?' he said a bit louder.

'London,' she answered.

'And Italy?' he questioned.

'Rome,' Nina answered sleepily.

'And of Greece?'

'Athens,' Nina said, and then, realising she had fallen straight into his trap, she threw her pillow at Alex's laughing head.

'Quiet in there!' Papa Papadopolos roared, and the twins giggled beneath their sheets.

5

The Song of the Afternoon

To celebrate the weekend, Mama Papadopolos liked to make ice cream on Fridays. She saved an egg a day all through the week, especially for the purpose of making the ice-cream custard. This Friday was no exception. When school ended and Mama had rested, she and Nina set about cracking and beating the eggs for the ice-cream custard. Alex was sent on his bicycle with the pull-along-cart attached, to fetch back a bag of ice-crystals from the factory. When the custard thickened, Mama put it in the fridge and said, 'now that's ready, all we need is your brother and the ice.'

Nina went outside. She walked down to the low wall at the end of their yard. It was still very hot even though it was late in the day. She stared out at the sea. It lay still and quiet. Across its wide surface tiny, silver ripples ran playfully after one another. Far away on the horizon Nina could see the small dot of the Blue Line fish-boat. It steamed towards Moutsouna, to make its daily collection of ice, before heading on for Athens. Nina kicked her feet in the dust and wondered about Athens. Should she write something about it in her book? She frowned. She had never been to Athens. What was the city really like? Could it really chew people up and spit them out, like Grandfather had said? She began to sing a song to comfort herself, a made-up song about the heat and the sea and making ice cream. A small lizard crawled up the wall beside her and she sang him into her song too.

Grandfather emerged from the house and shuffled to join her where she sat.

'Here comes the fish-boat,' he said and Nina looked up at him admiringly.

'Can you see it, Grandpa?' she asked.

'No,' he smiled. 'It's nearly four o'clock. It always comes about now. But this afternoon I can smell it.'

'Can you smell the fish?' Nina wanted to know.

'I can smell a lot of things today,' Grandfather said. 'I can smell a memory of the old days when the harbour was a flurry of boats all day long.'

'What sort of boats were they?' Nina asked her grandfather.

'All sorts, large and small. Every fisherman in the Aegean needed our ice in those days. There were crab boats from Crete and lobster boats from Lesbos. There were the eel men and the squid men. We made so much ice the whole harbour was cool. You could have worked right through the siesta if you'd wanted.'

'But now there's only the Blue Line fish-boat, only one boat that gets ice,' Nina said and she looked up to see it slowly steaming into the harbour.

'Progress,' the grandfather muttered crossly in a hoarse whisper. 'The biggest boat of all that one. Thirty years ago the Blue Line Company said it was the best thing to happen to fishing. Maybe so for them, but it put all the little boats out of business.'

'What else can you smell?' Nina asked quietly, taking her grandfather by the hand.

He sniffed the air and said nothing for a moment. Nina listened to the song of the afternoon, the sound of crickets and the small waves dancing on the beach.

At last the grandfather spoke.

'I smell something coming,' he said. 'There's a strong smell from the north.'

He sniffed again.

'It's a bad, bad smell,' he said finally and he stood up to go indoors.

6

Ice

Alex waited in the harbour beside his bicycle. He watched the great flock of white seagulls circling in the blue sky. Like him, they were waiting for the fish-boat. At length, practically on the dot of four o'clock, the great old fish-boat steamed into the little harbour. Like the ice-factory, the fish-boat was painted red with a blue stripe all around it, to signify the Blue Line Company which owned them both. As soon as the boat docked, the factory doors opened and the workers, led by Manager Marcos, spilled out.

Alex stood well back. He knew better than to get in Manager Marcos' way, but he watched him with round, curious eyes. Alex wondered what it was like to run a whole factory. Manager Marcos never seemed to be enjoying himself. He reminded Alex of Smelly Dimitri, the bad-tempered bus driver. Perhaps owning a factory made you grumpy, Alex thought, but he knew that Manager Marcos didn't actually own the ice-factory himself. He only ran it for the Blue Line Company. He had been sent especially from Athens and he lived alone in a small flat at the back of the factory. He had no children, no goats, no chickens and no olive trees. Alex wondered if that was why Manager Marcos didn't smile very often.

The huge boat docked and large ropes were thrown down and tied along the quay. The seagulls stopped circling to dive down in sharp arrows over the boat. Fishermen on board laughed at their antics and tossed unwanted fish heads and tails at them. The birds swooped down, shrieking joyfully as they caught food in mid-air or splashed into the harbour water to feast.

Manager Marcos blew a whistle and six massive ice-blocks were wheeled out of the factory onto the quay. It took four men to manoeuvre each one. Then the great clawed crane arm swung over and back, lifting the huge transparent blocks into the dark hold of the fish-boat.

When all the blocks had been loaded, a large shoot was swung out from the upstairs floor of the factory. It hovered over the massive fish-trays that lined the deck of the boat. At Manager Marcos' signal, sprays of tiny ice crystals cascaded from the shoot and in those moments when ice rained out of the sky, the harbour was filled with diamonds of light glinting with rainbows.

As soon as the ice-shoot was pulled back towards the factory, Alex cycled forward with his cart. Manager Marcos was used to Alex coming on a Friday. He knew the boy wanted ice and he knew it was to make ice cream with. Something that was nearly a smile came over his face. He held up his hand and signalled to the shoot operator, who swung the shoot over the quay until it hovered near Alex's bicycle. The man pulled a lever and a small cascade of crystals fell exactly into the pull-along-cart.

'Thank you!' Alex yelled, leaping onto his bicycle and turning to pedal away.

'Hey, wait a minute!' Manager Marcos shouted. 'Tell your mother, your father will be late home this evening. I've called a meeting of all the workers. I have something to tell them.'

'I will.' Alex nodded and he pedalled away as fast as he could, so as to get home before the ice melted.

7

The Ice-cream Makers

Nina was thinking about her book when Alex appeared around the corner shouting, 'Here I am, here's the ice!'

She was thinking about the ice-cream maker. She had decided it belonged in her book somewhere. The trouble was how to explain it to a person who had never seen such a thing. It was a very difficult task. Although the ice-cream maker was a very simple invention, actually telling someone how it worked might require a long explanation and she didn't want long explanations in her book.

'Wake up and help me, Nina!' Alex called as he parked by the porch and jumped from his bicycle. Together they began to scoop the ice into the ice compartment of the ice-cream maker. Mama came and poured the cream and the thick custard into the ice-cream compartment. Then they each measured in one spoon of chocolate powder.

They were about to put on the lid and begin the turning of the handle when a loud shout came from the scrubby bushes next door. The three of them turned around in time to see a flash of brown, goaty leg and Ios disappearing into the bushes.

Nina shook her head.

'That is the stubbornest goat in Greece.'

'The most stubborn goat in the whole world,' Alex said.

Mama laughed. The bushes waved and Ios shouted at Kalimara. The goat bleated and ran away. Ios puffed after her through the scrubby field.

'Come back here and be milked!' he yelled.

Alex and Mama and Nina turned away. It was the

same thing every day. Only when Ios had been pulled through enough bushes and shouted enough times, would he finally give up and throw his bucket to the ground. Only then would Kalimara come bleating behind him and allow herself be milked. A person had to give up and admit total defeat before that goat let you get on with things.

Alex screwed on the lid of the ice-cream maker tight and began to turn the handle of the machine. He turned and he turned and he turned. He turned the handle until his arm was hot and sore and he couldn't turn it another turn. Then Nina set to and had a go, but she didn't last very long. She was still thinking hard about how to explain the workings of the ice-cream machine and that meant she couldn't concentrate properly on the mixing. Mama Papadopolos rescued them both. Her strong brown arms could turn the handle for longer than either of the twins put together. She had been making ice cream her whole life long. She could remember making it with her mother and her grandmother before that, for the ice-cream maker had been in Mama's family for generations. Nobody, not even the blind grandfather, knew where it came from, but everybody in the village knew of it and wished that it were theirs.

Alex loved the ice-cream maker with all his heart. It was so simple. Of all the ways in the whole world of making ice cream, it surely was the easiest. All you needed was custard made from eggs, sugar and goat's milk, goat's cream and some sort of flavouring. You didn't need electricity, or a deep freeze. You only needed ice, and they had a whole factory of that, just down the road.

8

The Meeting

'Gentlemen I have good news,' Manager Marcos said, holding up his hands to silence the crowd of assembled ice-workers. 'Today is indeed an important day for the Blue Line Company. Thirty years ago we bought this ice-factory from the previous owner. For thirty years the good people of Moutsouna have been making ice for the Blue Line Company. In recognition of your hard work, the Blue Line is today giving this very factory to the good people of Moutsouna.'

A strange buzz of confusion went through the small crowd.

Papa Papadopolos stood beside Ios' father,

Pedros. 'What's he saying?' Papa asked. 'They're giving us the ice-factory? Why would they want to do that?'

Pedros shrugged his large shoulders. Manager Marcos continued talking despite the mixed reaction of his audience.

'You can set yourselves up as a workers' co-operative. Equal pay for everybody. I, myself shall be leaving at the end of next week.'

As the ice-workers listened to this last statement, the mood amongst them changed. Suddenly, they sensed something was wrong.

'Now, just a minute,' Papa Papadopolos yelled from the back of the crowd. 'You had better explain yourself better.'

'Yes!' The other workers shouted, 'Explain yourself better. What's going on?'

Manager Marcos began to look uncomfortable, but bravely he stammered, 'This very day in Athens ...'

Papa Papadopolos felt the hairs on the back of

his neck stand up. Why did everybody have to keep on about Athens all the time?

'This very day,' Manager Marcos said, raising his voice above the heckling crowd, 'the Blue Line Company is launching a new ship. It is the most modern fishing boat in the whole world. It is capable of catching thousands of tonnes of fish in a day. Not only that, gentlemen, but this wonderful ship has every kind of refrigeration and processing equipment already aboard. Within minutes of those fish being caught, they can be transformed into fish fingers. They can even be packaged in boxes and stamped with price tags. That's how marvellous this new ship is.'

'Marvellous!' Someone in the crowd echoed approvingly.

'Marvellous?' Papa Papadopolos shouted. 'Don't you see what this means? Don't you see what's going on? It's a trick. They are giving us the factory because they don't need it any more. They don't need the old fish-boat, they don't need ice and they don't need ice-workers!'

Now the crowd understood.

'Gentlemen, calm yourselves,' Manager Marcos tried. 'The Blue Line Company always looks after its workers. Tomorrow I shall be giving out one month's pay to each and every man amongst you. Within a month you will have worked out how to best run the ice-factory and you'll be able to pay yourselves wages once again.'

At this Papa Papadopolos went bright red in the face.

'Nonsense!' he bellowed. 'We only make ice for the Blue Line Company. They are the only people in the whole Aegean Sea that need ice. Don't you see, there won't be any wages in a month, because with this new ship there'll be nobody left to buy our ice ...' Papa Papadopolos was practically spitting. He could barely get the words out of his mouth. The other workers were equally lost; they looked to one another with blank fearful faces.

'Gentlemen, I'm sure you'll manage,' Manager

Marcos said nervously. 'If not, you can always apply for jobs on the new fish-boat.' He smiled anxiously and hurried from the factory before the ice-workers had time to turn against him.

9

Deep-fried Squid

At home, things were not going well either. Alex, in his excitement over the ice-cream making, had forgotten to tell Mama about the meeting at the factory. Not realising that he would be late home, Mama Papadopolos had spent ages preparing Papa's favourite dish: deep-fried squid. It was only when Mama triumphantly brought the steaming food to the table, that Alex remembered Manager Marcos' message.

Mama was furious! She might ordinarily have forgiven Alex and told them all to get on and eat without Papa, but her nerves were already frayed by Grandfather's behaviour. He had spent the whole evening sniffing and snuffling about the kitchen like a dog that has forgotten where it buried a bone. He sat now, at the kitchen table, muttering to himself.

'Sniff. Could be a fight of some kind ... a feud ... sniff ... no ... it's softer, darker and oh, it's bad ... it's a bad smell ... it's rotten ...'

'Please Grandpa,' Mama said gently, 'could you stop now?'

Grandfather was too preoccupied; he had not even noticed the arrival of the squid which was rapidly going cold, nor had he noticed Mama's bad mood. She laid her hand on the old man's arm.

'Please father, you are frightening the children. Can you talk about something else?'

The old man looked confused. Mama had plucked him from his dark world back into the kitchen.

'I'm sorry, Eleni,' he said. 'I'm sorry, but the stench is terrible. I don't think I can eat anything. My nose is too full.' With that he excused himself and shuffled sadly to his bedroom.

The twins were left with their mother and the plate of soggy, cold squid. Mama looked as if she might cry. An awful silence filled the room. Nobody said anything, but at last Alex could not bear the mood for another second.

'Where's the Statue of Liberty, Nina?' he burst out.

'New York,' she hissed quietly, for she was nervous and worried about Mama.

'And the Sydney Opera House?'

'Sydney, of course.' She glared at her brother.

'Yes, of course. What about the Eiffel tower?'

'That's in Paris.'

'And the Coliseum?'

'Rome,' Mama Papadopolos answered despite herself.

'And the Leaning Tower?'

'Pisa!' Mama and Nina chanted together.

'And the Acropolis?' Alex asked as the front door swung open and a very pale, white-faced Papa

Papadopolos walked in. Too late to even stop themselves, Mama and Nina shouted out the one word that triggered Papa Papadopolos falling to the floor with a terrific crash.

'Athens!'

10

Not a Melon

In his fall Papa Papadopolos had blackened his left eye and broken a small chunk from a front tooth. Now when he said the letters 'S' and 'N' and 'X', a strange whistle escaped through the gap in his teeth.

Throughout breakfast the next morning, he gradually spoke less and less and when he did so it was mostly to Mama or Grandfather, because he could neither say Nina or Alex without whistling his strange new tune.

Nobody spoke much. They were all too worried about the news from the ice-factory. Silence hovered above them, turning the room sour.

'We must smile at this, Papa,' Mama finally broke

in. 'You are always telling the children to smile at life, to welcome whatever comes.'

'Yes,' said Grandfather, 'somehow or other we must smile at this as if we were Filipos Velcanos and this disaster were nothing more than a herd of stray goats or a stubborn donkey, or a woman with more children and parcels than she can carry.'

'That's right,' Mama said. 'That's what you've always told the children. We must smile as if this were nothing more than dropped melons or a broken-down tourist ...'

Papa Papadopolos leapt to his feet. He towered over Nina and Alex, looking completely wild.

'Smile?' he shouted and whistled at the same time. 'How can I smile? This is not a broken-down donkey or a stray tourist or a stubborn melon. This is not a goat carrying too many children. Don't you know what this is? This means only one thing. This is Athens!' He thundered, and the whistle that sprang through his teeth was like an alarm bell ringing through the whole house.

11

Discovering Athens

After that things changed in Moutsouna. Most of the village children carried on swimming in the sea and playing football on the beach as they had always done. Their mothers, along with Mama Papadopolos, gathered together in each other's kitchens to talk and share their concerns. The fathers, the former ice-workers, filled with despair and overcome with worry for the future, took to their beds and refused to move. Alone, Alex roamed the empty ice-factory, investigating the various machines, which stood still and silent. But the blind grandfather and Nina went to the library in Apiranthos, to find a guidebook about their capital city.

All through the following days tempers were thin in the Papadopolos household. Alex stayed away as much as he could, spending nearly all his time at the factory. Mama tried to carry on with life as normal, but things were not normal. Papa was still in bed. He said his feet couldn't move, because they knew if they started walking again they'd only be headed for Athens and they weren't ready for the journey yet. Mama was furious. In front of the children she'd called Papa a coward and ordered him to get up at once, but Papa either couldn't or wouldn't get out of bed.

Grandfather and Nina sat at the kitchen table reading their guidebook. This irritated Mama to the point of distraction. In a fury she dragged the kitchen table into Papa's room and sent Grandfather and Nina along with it.

Grandfather didn't mind being shunted into the bedroom. He was very disappointed with Papa Papadopolos. He thought Papa ought to be taking steps to protect his family from the impending disaster. So when Papa asked them to go away and read elsewhere the grandfather ignored him, encouraging Nina to read a little louder.

'The beginning bit again, Nina,' he instructed, pretending he was deaf instead of blind. In a loud, clear voice Nina read:

'Chapter one, "Discovering Athens. Athens lies close to the west coast of the Attic Peninsula, almost in the centre of Greece. It is a big sprawling city, housing over five million people." That's a lot of people, isn't it Grandpa?'

'A bit bigger than Moutsouna.' The grandfather nodded.

Nina continued, "'It is easy to get to Athens because there are now two airports and Athens' sprawling suburbs join up with the busy shipping-port of Piraeus. In summer the city is dirty, noisy, hot and covered in an unhealthy cloud of pollution called the Nefos."'

'Dirty, noisy, hot and covered in the Nefos, eh?'

the grandfather repeated. 'That's bad, eh? But there must be beaches. Tell me about the beaches, Nina.'

Again Nina bent her head into the book.

'It says, "There are no beaches in Athens and none fit to swim from within kilometres of the port of Piraeus because of pollution." But where will we swim every day?' Nina asked sadly.

'Hm,' Grandfather said, 'you may not be able to go swimming any more. But at least there's the Acropolis and the Parthenon to look at instead. I bet they'll be worth seeing.'

'Listen to this, Grandpa,' Nina said enthusiastically. 'It says here there's a Tower of the Winds. "Built in the first century by an astronomer, this octagonal tower is a sundial, weather vane, water clock and compass."'

Even Papa Papadopolos sat up in bed, sounding interested. 'Alex would like an invention like that. A sundial, weather vane, water clock and compass?' he queried.

'That's what it says,' Nina answered.

'Interesting,' Papa said, brightening for a minute, and then a dark cloud settled back around him and he sank into his pillows.

'Never,' he muttered. 'Never.'

12

Ice Dreams

Alex lolled at the end of the bed, trying to get his head comfortable on his father's legs. Nina lay squashed in between her parents. The twins were aware their mother wasn't speaking to their father and their father wasn't talking to their mother. A pair of flies buzzed in circles beneath the ceiling lamp. At last, when Nina could stand the silence no longer, she said, 'Will we really have to move to Athens?'

Mama sighed. Papa let out a small groan but neither said anything. Secretly Mama was waiting to see what Papa would say and Papa was waiting for Mama to come up with her answer.

'Of course not,' Alex shook his head. 'We'll think of something.'

Papa smiled at his son. 'Dear Alex,' he said, 'I wish we could think of something, but what can we do? Without the ice-factory Moutsouna has nothing. A village cannot survive on olive trees and chickens any more. Things are more complicated nowadays.'

'But Papa, we don't just have olive trees and chickens. We have eggs and milk and cream,' Alex interrupted.

'And melons and lemons,' Nina joined in.

'And boats to fish from,' Alex said.

'Small boats,' Papa sighed.

'And we still have the ice-factory. We could get it going again,' Alex said quite crossly.

'Yes, but nobody wants ice any more. The Blue Line Company was our only customer. There's no point making ice if nobody is going to buy it,' Papa said, trying to be patient.

'Couldn't we make something else in the ice

factory?' Nina asked. 'Couldn't we turn it into a toy-factory or something?'

Papa took a deep breath. 'To run a factory you need two things. You need machinery and materials. If you want to make toys you need machines that make toys and you need a supply of wood or metal or plastic. We can't get the ice-factory going as some other sort of factory because we only have machines that make ice and we have no materials.'

'We could have fish,' Nina suggested. 'If we sent everybody fishing we might catch enough to make fish fingers.'

'Yes, but we could never make them as cheaply as the Blue Line Company. Our fish fingers would be very expensive and nobody wants to buy expensive fish fingers. That's the other thing you need if you're going to have a factory. You need a space in the market. You need a certain amount of people who'll buy what you make at your price. That's basic economics,' Papa said, getting flustered.

'Frozen olives?' Nina suggested.

Papa gave her a tired look and then he smiled and ruffled her hair.

'My dear daughter, I don't think anybody wants to eat frozen olives. You store olives in olive oil. Greece is full of olive factories. It doesn't need another one. No, we must accept our situation is hopeless, totally hopeless.'

'So we shall go to Athens?' Nina asked.

Papa hissed and Mama turned over to stare at the cupboard by the bed as if she were thinking of all the things they would have to pack up and take with them. The room filled with a horrible silence.

Then Alex sat up. He took a deep breath. He said, 'At the ice factory there are six, big, round machines. In the centre of each are large blades that go round and round.'

'Yes,' Papa sighed. 'The crushers. Those were the machines that made tiny ice crystals. The constant freezing, combined with the turning blades meant that the ice could only ever form into small crystals, instead of large blocks.'

'Well,' Alex said, hurrying his words out, 'if you cut the blades in half and built a canister of some sort around them, you'd have an ice-cream maker.'

'An electric ice-cream maker?' Nina shouted. 'You mean you wouldn't have to turn the handle all afternoon?'

'An ice-cream maker?' Papa queried.

'Just like Mama's, but electric,' Alex said triumphantly. 'And we have the materials for ice cream. We have eggs and cream and ice.'

For a minute Papa smiled.

'Our own ice-cream factory, eh?' he said.

'And there's a market. Nobody in the whole island of Naxos makes ice cream. They ship it here on boats from Athens,' Alex said, standing up and waving his arms happily.

Nina jumped up and bounced down to the end of the bed beside her brother. 'See, there is an answer! We've got chickens to make eggs and goats for cream ...'

'We could make chocolate ice cream,' Alex sang.

'And lemon ice-pops,' Nina said, leaping and falling on Papa's legs.

'And melon lollies,' Alex laughed.

'Stop!' Papa shouted 'Stop! Stop at once!'

'But don't you think it's a good idea, Papa?' Alex asked sadly.

'It's a good idea, yes, but it's a ridiculous idea. It's a dream. We have a handful of eggs and a jug of cream, we don't have enough ...'

'But if all the people of Moutsouna saved their eggs and their cream,' Alex suggested.

Mama smiled. 'Yes, then it would work,' she said.

'Of course it wouldn't. Don't be ridiculous! Don't raise the children's hopes! It could never work. Never in a million years,' Papa said very crossly.

'Why not?' Mama asked defiantly.

Papa went silent. Of course it couldn't work. 'It's a dream, an ice dream. Don't be silly. The factory is dead; it's over.'

'No! The children are right,' Mama said, her eyes bright with enthusiasm and daring. She jumped out of bed. 'We have ice. We have cream and eggs and flavours. We have a market. We've got everything we need.'

Suddenly a thought bubbled up in Papa's mind.

'Sugar! It won't work because you don't have any sugar!'

Mama frowned at him and stamped her foot on the ground. However angry she had been with Papa before, now she was really fuming.

'Sugar is a minor detail and you know it. Come on children, we've work to do,' she said, pulling Alex and Nina out of the room, leaving Papa all alone in his bed.

13

Mama Starts Thinking

Mama took the children to the factory. She made Alex show her the ice-crushers. He explained how they could be altered so as to become exact replicas of the ice-cream maker. Mama looked at them and then she looked at her son and she smiled proudly.

'You're right Alex, you're quite right.'

Then she took a tour of the whole factory, asking Alex to explain everything he knew. At last she led them back out into the bright sun.

'We've got to do some thinking. We need to think

fast, we haven't got much time,' Mama said, leading Alex and Nina over to the quay. They sat down on the edge between the big iron rings that would have held the ropes for the ice-boat when it docked.

'We'll have to make a list of everything we need,' Mama said, holding up her fingers, beginning to count as if she was making a shopping-list. Finger by finger she listed aloud the following: eggs, cream, flavouring, sugar, machinery, packaging, transport, workers, goodwill and luck.

'We only need ten things,' Mama smiled. 'It might just work.'

Beside her Alex thought about the things on Mama's list. Eggs and cream and flavouring would be easy enough, but Papa was right, they didn't have sugar. Nor did they have quite the right machines yet. There certainly had no way to transport frozen ice cream even if they had any packaging to put it in. At the moment all the ice-workers were still in bed; it might take more than goodwill to get them up again. Alex hung his legs over the edge of the dock

and swung them thoughtfully. He decided they were going to need an awfully large amount of luck.

For a while nobody said anything as they each thought about how difficult it might actually be to make an ice-cream factory. Perhaps Papa was right; perhaps it was impossible.

'It's very quiet without the fish-boat,' Alex said at last. 'This time of day used to be a circus.'

It was true. The afternoon seemed very silent, the harbour empty except for a black cat that came and rubbed its face against Nina's legs.

'No fish today, Puss,' Nina said, and the cat yowled hungrily.

'Poor cat,' Mama said.

'The cat will be fine,' Alex said. 'Someone will feed him. It's the seagulls I'm worried about. They used to come here every day and the men threw scraps from the fish-boat. I haven't seen a seagull for days.'

At once Mama and Nina scanned the harbour. They looked up into the wide blue sky and out over the silver sea. Alex was right; there wasn't a bird to be seen.

'Where have they all gone, Mama?' Nina asked sadly.

'Oh, don't worry,' Mama said, trying to sound more cheerful than she felt. 'They're seagulls; they hunt for their own food.'

'But what if they had nests somewhere with babies in them? Maybe they depended on the ice-boat just like us?' Nina questioned worriedly.

Mama tried to soothe her, 'It's not the right season for baby birds. I'm sure the seagulls will be safe. They've probably flown off to some other port full of boats and nets and fish-heads being thrown overboard.'

'But Grandfather says progress got rid of all the little fishing-boats. What if there aren't any ports anymore, what then?' Nina pleaded, staring out to sea, imagining the poor seagulls flying on and on without finding food or shelter.

'Well,' Alex said matter-of-factly, 'they'll have to

do what everyone else in the islands has to do. They'll have to move to Athens.'

'But what if they don't want to go? What if they liked Moutsouna?' Nina said with a deep sigh. The black cat at her feet looked up and gave a long, mournful wail.

14

Mama Holds a Meeting

Mama invited the whole village. The children came, wide-eyed and excited, already fired up with rumours they had heard about an ice-cream factory. The women of the village came, wide-eyed and nervous, their hearts already full of a week's worry. The grandparents and the old men and women of the village came, wide-eyed and enthusiastic, determined to help Mama Papadopolos with her plan. Filipos the bus driver came and stood at the back of the porch smiling at everyone. Only the men stayed away, the ice-workers, without whom the whole plan would not be possible. They stayed in their beds, even Papa Papadopolos would not attend.

Bravely, Mama explained the plan. She said she needed help. She said, with a bit of luck and everybody's goodwill, they had a chance of success. The people were not sure what to think, but Mama told them they didn't have to be sure just yet. All they had to do was start saving an egg a day, and from Monday onwards, they would need to save their cream. Mama Papadopolos begged them not to use their sugar.

She told the women to come with their saved eggs and their saved cream and their saved sugar to the factory next Thursday morning. It had to be next Thursday she explained, so that they could sell the ice cream in the market on Friday morning in Naxos Town.

She asked the grandparents and the old uncles and aunts if they could help by looking after the children and she asked the children if they could help by collecting up every old yoghurt pot and plastic container they could find. She said they'd also need to gather clean twigs for spoons and ice-lolly sticks.

At school Mama said the same thing to the children of Apiranthos. Very soon a mountain of containers began to grow. At the end of school on Monday and on Wednesday, Filipos helped Mama and the twins load them into the bus. He drove the bus all the way back down the hairpin-bend road to Mama's front door where he helped unload carton after carton and pot after pot. Then the village women gathered to wash the containers and talk about how the plan was coming along. Once they had the plastic pots clean and dry, Mama stored them in the bedroom. She lined them up against the walls in stacks, moving them closer and closer to where Papa lay in bed. Mama ignored Papa's cross remarks. She was too angry with him to answer back. Besides, as the days passed, she was growing more and more nervous. The people of Moutsouna and even the people of Apiranthos, who had heard everything from their children, were becoming more and more excited. Everyone wanted to know if the plan could possibly work and Mama felt responsible. What on earth would happen if it failed?

15

The Most Stubborn Goat in the Whole Country

'Alex, we're running out of time. Could you invent a way to get Papa out of bed?' Mama asked on Tuesday afternoon.

'I could try,' Alex shrugged. 'I don't know how though.'

'Neither do I,' Mama said. 'I've already tried everything I can think of. It's the same stubbornness in every house. The men think our plan will never work. They'd rather we handed them tickets to Athens. The only person who'll help is Filipos. He's happy to carry the ice cream on the bus, if we can work out how to keep it cool.'

'But Mama, it's two hours to Naxos Town. Ice cream won't stand a chance! Even if you drove at night, it would be soup before you reached Apiranthos.'

'We'll think of something. Transport is the least of our worries. If we don't have ice, we won't have ice cream. We need Papa up and out of bed today. Invent something, please,' Mama said desperately. She gave Alex a big hug and then went outside to feed the chickens.

Alex thought for a while. He knew if he had enough time and enough tools, he could invent a machine that would be strong enough to pull Papa Papadopolos out of bed. But no machine could make him do things once he was upright. If he worked at it, Alex might be able to invent a reason to get Papa out of bed, but what better reason was there than the threat of moving to Athens? Feeling lost and defeated, Alex followed his mother out of the house. The sea glistened invitingly. Alex thought how good it would be to go swimming in the cool, clear water. But he had inventing to do: how to get Papa out of bed?

Suddenly, there was an outburst of shouting from the scrubby field behind Ios' house next door. Ios was trying to milk Kalimara. Alex watched the bushes thrashing about as Ios hastily pursued Kalimara.

'Come back here!' Ios shouted, but as usual it did no good.

Alex laughed to himself as he watched their performance. The bushes waved wildly until at last, Alex heard the crash of a metal milk bucket land on dry earth.

'Milk yourself, you stubborn donkey!' Ios yelled, not caring who heard him, as he stomped back towards the house.

A minute later Kalimara had picked the bucket up in her mouth and was trotting after Ios. It was in that moment that Alex had his invention.

16

The Most Stubborn Donkey in the Whole World

The twins and their grandfather listened at the door when Mama went in to Papa's room a short time later. They did not dare to look at each other in case they got the giggles. And besides it wasn't really funny. Nina and Alex and their grandfather all knew how serious things had become. If Mama failed to get Papa out of bed, the ice-cream factory was going to be a dream that they remembered as they sat beneath the Nefos in Athens.

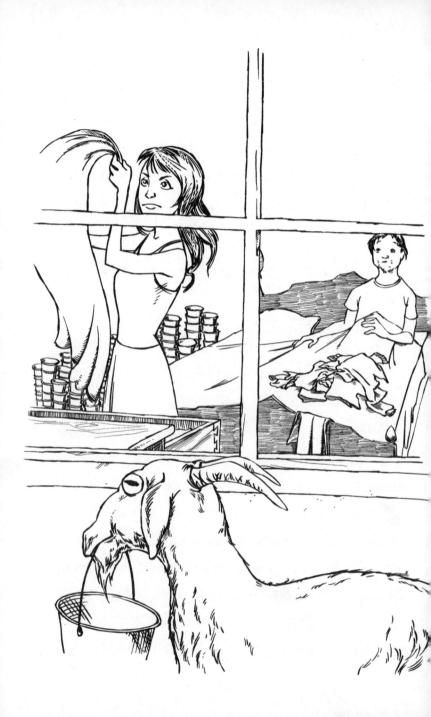

'You're right, Papa,' Mama said as she swept into the room and aimed straight for the chest of drawers where Papa kept his clothes. She opened a drawer and began taking out all Papa's underpants.

'It never would have worked,' she exclaimed, throwing them onto the bed where they landed across Papa's legs. She loaded her arms with socks and turned to toss them on the bed. Then Mama crossed the room towards the cupboard, throwing a last pair of socks over her shoulder. They hit Papa on the nose and then bounced to the floor, knocking over a stack of plastic cartons.

'Much better not to try,' Mama said, opening the cupboard and knocking over another two piles. She began taking out Papa's trousers. She folded them neatly in half.

'What?' Papa asked. 'What am I right about?'

'This whole ice-cream idea!' Mama answered, spilling a basket of her underwear onto Papa's covers.

'What?' Papa asked again as Mama dived down

under the bed and began throwing pairs of shoes out from underneath.

'I mean,' she said, emerging red-faced, 'how could it work? We've no sugar, we've no cold transport. Besides, who on earth would want to eat home-made, handmade ice-cream? Ridiculous idea altogether.' She disappeared back into the cupboard and brought out her shirts and skirts. Papa watched her, confused and uncertain.

'You're packing,' he said.

'Indeed I am. And I'm sorry to have wasted so much time on this silly pipe-dream. The sooner we're packed the better,' Mama exclaimed.

'But ...' Papa said incredulous. 'But ...' He frowned.

'You were right all along. I should have listened. I'm sorry I was so stubborn. I'm the most stubborn goat in the whole country,' Mama said, going back to the cupboard and pulling out her special red dress. For a moment she looked at it. It was her best dress, the one she always wore on birthdays and to weddings, the one she wore on the rare occasions she and Papa went to the small cinema in Apiranthos. Yes, she thought sadly, it was Papa's favourite dress too. And it was the red dress hanging from her arm like a bull fighter's cloak which finally awoke Papa.

'Stop, stop!' he cried, leaping up out of bed, knocking a stack of plastic pots flying as he raced across the room to Mama. Suddenly he didn't know what to say. 'Not the red dress,' he said foolishly.

Mama looked at the dress in her hands. She began to fold it up as if she were packing it in a suitcase.

'Only a silly idea from the start,' Mama said, 'just a dream.'

'No,' Papa said, taking the dress from her. And suddenly, feeling it in his hands, he knew it meant everything that was good and right about their lives. 'What about the children? We can't disappoint them. We can't just give up now. No, Eleni, no, it's a wonderful idea. What's a little sugar or transport? We've got ice, tonnes of ice and we'll buy sugar,'

Papa said, pushing Mama's red dress back into the cupboard.

'But the machines aren't ready. They need welding. It won't work,' Mama said, taking the dress out again.

'I'll fix the machines. Of course, it'll work,' Papa answered, taking the dress back.

'It's not that simple,' Mama said, tugging the red dress away from him and knocking over another pile of pots.

'Oh yes, it is that simple, Papa said, raising his voice just a little, and in one quick movement he put his arms around Mama and the favourite dress.

'I'm sorry Eleni,' he whispered. 'I've been very foolish. I've been the most stubborn donkey in the whole world. I've wasted a lot of time. But it's not too late, is it?' he asked.

Mama looked at Papa's wild, unshaven face, his unbrushed hair and his fiery passionate eyes.

'No,' she said softly, 'it's not too late.'

17

Moutsouna Wakes Up

After that it was as if everyone woke up from a long sleep. The village became a hive of activity with people buzzing from one place to another. As soon as the men heard that Papa Papadopolos was down at the ice-factory fixing up the ice-crushers, they all got out of their beds as if they had never even been in them. Papa and Alex, together with the help of Ios and his father, Pedros, made alterations to the ice-crushers. They cut and welded, and cut and welded metal right through the siesta in their hurry to get the job finished. The other men turned to the ice-machines with a new zeal, and as the freezers began to hum and throb once more, a special song of hope rang through the village.

Everyone began working together. The children hunted through the olive groves, gathering short thin twigs for ice lollies and long, flat sticks for spoons. The grandmothers whittled the bark from them and washed them and the grandfathers sat about carving little spoons with pocket-knives that had not been used for many years. Uncles who had not fished for years went out in small boats to bring home food. Fathers who had only previously made ice were now busy at the command of Filipos constructing boxes and frames to strap onto the bus so the ice cream could travel to Naxos Town in safety. There was a flurry and a purpose about the whole village. On a bench in the harbour, Nina sat with the grandfather, telling him everything that she could see going on. As she watched the people of Moutsouna hurry about their business, a small tiny thought fluttered in her like a secret: maybe this, all this, was what she was supposed to be writing about in her book. But when? There was so much going on, and so much to do, and never any time for writing.

When the famous Thursday dawned to the familiar crows of faithful cockerels, the villagers were already awake and making their way to the ice-factory. Mama Papadopolos had allowed the children the day off from school and now she stood in the centre of the factory, telling everyone what to do. She had a team of workers making custard, another making ice, another cleaning the empty yoghurt pots for one final time and another team cooking food for the workers on a giant barbecue set up on the quay. Nina and Alex ran about from one team to another looking over the work, trying to put their fingers into the mixtures and begging for a taste. But Mama had made a list of rules: the children were not allowed to try anything; only Mama and her special testing

spoon were allowed near the mixtures. Alex and Nina were sent out with the other children into the harbour to help set up tables and chairs for the evening meal.

By the time evening fell every pot had been filled. There was vanilla ice cream and chocolate ice cream, there was melon sorbet and lemon sorbet, and there were ice lollies of assorted shapes and sizes, depending on the type of recycled pot that had been used as a mould.

At sunset the whole village sat down to eat together. They were so hungry and tired that no one said anything until Alex heard a familiar squawking behind him. He turned around to see a family of seagulls circling on the evening air.

'Look, Mama, look!' he shouted and everyone craned their heads upwards. At once a great burst of laughter and chatter broke out amongst the villagers. Nina clapped her hands for joy. She hugged Mama and ran to sit on Papa's knee. For the rest of the evening she stayed there, watching the talk and laughter, music and dancing, thinking to herself that tomorrow she would write all this down. Here, right under her nose, was the story she needed to put in her book!

18

The Ice-bus

On Friday morning the children rode to school on a bus laden with ice. It looked like a double-decker bus now that it wore a roof rack and a special frame to hold the massive ice-blocks in place around its precious ice-cream cargo. But despite the fact Filipos was driving nobody chanted 'Apiranthos, Apiranthos!' as they rounded the fierce bends. There was a tense quiet, a hush, as if nobody dared breathe or make a sound in case it made the ice melt or fall from where it had been fixed in place. The village children rode all the way to school in Apiranthos in complete silence. They whispered goodbye and good luck to Papa Papadopolos,

Pedros, Alex and Ios who had been chosen to sell the ice cream in the market. Nina gave a last sad wave as the bus swung out of the village square, wishing that she too could be on board. Understanding her feelings, Mama squeezed her hand and walked with her to school.

Papa, Pedros, Ios and Alex sat right behind Filipos, anxiously watching the road ahead. At every bend they held their breath in case ice fell and every time the bus stopped for passengers they tapped their feet impatiently as if it might help the people climb aboard more quickly. At Filoti a crowd of people heading for Naxos market stepped in. They knew nothing about the closure of the ice-factory and the trouble in Moutsouna, nor about the ice-cream dream. But before long they knew all about it. Soon the people in Halki and the people in Galanado knew. As the bus descended onto the plains, it began to look like a moving car wash; drops of water ran down the windows and flew off the sides as it hurtled over the dusty road. So soon the people who lived on the plains knew too.

Inside the bus was unusually cool, which the passengers liked, for by the time the bus came off the plains, it was full and overcrowded. Ios and Alex had to sit on their father's laps, while people in the aisle stood and swayed between bags of melons and bags of lemons and baskets of chickens ready to be sold in the market. Everyone talked of nothing else but the wicked Blue Line Company and the ice dream and when at last the bus unloaded in crowded Naxos Town, there was a rush of bus passengers attempting to be first in the queue for Moutsouna Ice Cream.

19

Ingredients

They sold every last drop. There wasn't even any spare for Alex and Ios. They had to make do with the big crusty sandwiches their fathers had made that morning. Enviously, they watched the children of Naxos Town walk away with their lollies and their pots and their wooden spoons.

At the end of the afternoon the boys climbed back onto Filipos' bus, tired and happy and glad to be heading home. Alex snuggled against his father and shut his eyes. His head was a whirl of pictures from the market: fruit and vegetables, people and animals, fish and meat and noise. All day he had listened to Papa and Pedros selling ice cream. All day people had said, 'Mm, yes, but what's in it?' And all day Papa had said, 'it's handmade, home-made ice cream. There's nothing but the best of cream and eggs, sugar and fruit.' Now, as the empty bus jolted and the engine started, Alex thought about all the things that had happened.

He thought about all the ingredients in their ice cream, all the eggs laid by the dusty chickens, which each day were fed and tended by the mothers of Moutsouna. He smiled when he thought of all the different village goats that had given their milk; he grinned especially hard when he thought of stubborn Kalimara. He thought too of the huge green melons that he'd watched swell through the long summer and he thought of the bright shiny lemons from the trees in the back yards. He thought of how the people had gone without sugar and he thought of all the arms that had beaten the custard and the wrinkled hands of the old people that had carved the little wooden spoons. He knew that everybody in the whole village had done something or said

something or made something that had helped make the ice cream. He tugged on Papa's sleeve.

'Papa, you could never list all the ingredients that went into our ice cream, could you?'

Papa put his arm around Alex's small shoulder and squeezed.

'No, my son, you could never list them all, but I think you can taste them,' he said, pulling out a small bag in which nestled two last pots that he had hidden away earlier on. He handed one to Pedros to share with Ios. 'You can taste all the things people did or said or gave. That's why it's so delicious. That's why everybody wants to buy more.'

20

We Need More Time

Nina chewed on the end of her pencil. It tasted woody. She wrinkled her nose and frowned. She breathed out a long deep sigh. She bit her lip. She sucked on her pencil once more, and frowned again. No, it was no good. No matter how hard Nina tried to write down her story, the words wouldn't come. It was too hot and the afternoon was too long, and it was too hard trying to write, what with all the waiting for Alex and Papa to return. Nina heard a noise outside her window. She jumped up to look, but it was only two children rolling a huge melon down the road toward the harbour. They were headed for the evening barbeque, laughing with one another and giggling every time the melon steered out of control. Nina went and sat back at the table. She picked up her pencil. She tried again. But it really was no good. How could she write anything when the future of Moutsouna was so uncertain? How could she write anything when a huge melon had to be rolled all the way to the harbour? She couldn't write a book with so much going on. Nina dropped her pencil and ran outside shouting to the children to wait for her help.

By the time the melon reached its destination, the evening barbeque was ready, the villagers had gathered, and the ice-bus was back in the harbour! Nina ran to join her Papa. She had to push her way through the crowd of people swarming around him, eager for news. Nina squirmed through legs and squeezed between bodies until she was right beside him, and Papa was scooping her up into his arms.

'Today was a great day,' Papa shouted, planting a big kiss on Nina's cheek. 'Today was one of the finest days in the whole history of Moutsouna. We succeeded. We sold every last drop of Moutsouna Ice Cream.'

The crowd cheered.

Papa gave Nina a squeeze, then gently he let her slide down to the ground.

'The trouble is,' Papa began, and his voice grew slow and serious, 'for this to work, we need more time.' He hung his head and drew a deep breath. Nina stood shyly beside her Papa. She clung to his hand, running her small fingers over the big black hairs on his wrist for comfort. 'For this to really get going,' Papa hesitated, 'we need to produce more ice cream and for that we need more chickens and more goats. Until we have more animals things are going to be very difficult, we're going to have to do without.'

Nina felt the atmosphere change around them. Like everyone in the village she knew the only way to get more chickens was to allow a broody hen to sit on a clutch of eggs. She knew that a broody hen needed to sit on her eggs for twenty-one whole days before the tiny fluffy feathers of chicks appeared, and she knew all too well how long it would take before the tiny fluffy chicks were old enough to lay their own eggs. Goats were even worse. For a goat to have a kid, and a kid to grow old enough to have kids itself and make milk was longer than the time between one olive harvest and the next.

Papa Papadopolos spoke again, 'We're going to have to tighten our belts.'

Nina looked down at her trousers and saw she wasn't wearing a belt. She looked at Papa, but he was speaking out to the disappointed villagers.

'We're going to have to do without. Save every last penny we can. Save electricity. It might be weeks or months before we make a go of this. It's time to unplug our radios and hair-dryers, to stop using our fridges. We've got to drink water and eat plain food every day, until ... until ...' Papa's voice trailed away. The trouble was, he couldn't say until when; no one knew how long this might take, or indeed whether it really could work, really work well enough to support a whole village.

Nina could see the worried faces of her friends and neighbours. They were all turned towards Papa in sorrow. It was as if they had all believed that selling the ice cream in the market would be a magic wand. As if that alone would be enough to save the village. Now Papa was telling them things were going to be difficult for a long while.

'This is a time for us to pull together. We can do it. We'll all be fine,' Papa reassured them, but it was too late for reassurance. The people had begun to fret. They turned to one another helplessly, their faces full of doubt.

Papa's hands began to shake a little. Nina tried to comfort him, but she didn't know what to say. It was obvious that this strange, tense and busy time would carry on until who knew when? Nina shook her head slowly. It wasn't just the fate of the village that was so uncertain. It was obvious that until things calmed down she wasn't going to have the chance to write her book. Suddenly there was a loud noise from the road. A rusty old van swung into the harbour. It came to a juddering halt just by the barbeque. Then another van swung into the harbour. Behind it came a car and another car and then a seemingly endless train of vehicles, motorbikes and bicycles, even the village bus, driven by Smelly Dimitri Simitos. Suddenly, there were people everywhere and as they got out of their vans and cars and clambered from the bus, the air filled with the bleating of goats and the squawking of chickens. From inside one rusty old van came the triumphant crow of a cockerel.

'People of Moutsouna,' Smelly Dimitri shouted, 'we the people of Apiranthos and the people of Filoti and Halki, we want to help you. We have gathered all that we can spare, every last goat and chicken that we can do without, and we give them to you now, with our wishes for the success of your ice-cream factory!'

Papa opened his hands in a big shrug as if he

didn't understand. Then Mama stood up and said, 'Thank you!' Then everyone was standing up and saying thank you and all the people and children were moving around amongst the squawking chickens and the bleating goats, shaking hands with one another, exchanging stories and jokes and news.

Nina just stood watching, smiling at Alex who was chasing after a runaway goat and laughing out loud.

21

Nina's Book

So it was that the people of the island of Naxos began to appear daily in Moutsouna. From every nook and cranny they came, for they had heard the story of the ice-factory and they knew the history of their islands. They brought whatever that had to spare. At last they had a chance to help stop the endless drift of islanders to the mainland and the city of Athens. They brought chickens and goats, empty plastic pots, cheese and bread and olives; in short they brought whatever they thought might help. One man brought a sack of oranges. Mama divided them between the ice-cream factory and the village children. Someone else brought charcoal and someone else brought wine. By degrees Moutsouna became a popular place to be. Children all over the island begged their parents to bring them to the famous ice-dream factory to sample the delicious ice cream. Moutsouna became something of an island attraction. Visitors swam in the sea and there were legendary football games on the beach. The bright young people of Naxos Town arrived in the evenings to gossip and chatter and dance on the beach and they left early in the mornings, just as the old people of Apiranthos and Filoti and Halki were climbing off the bus with their arms full of knitting and advice and encouragement.

Business was always brisk in the market on Fridays in Naxos Town. Moutsouna Ice Cream sold out before the market was over. It wasn't long before the hotel owners from the beaches outside Naxos Town came to the village to order ice cream for their restaurants. With them came the foreign tourists, people from Germany and France, from England and Ireland and beyond. They had their photographs taken in front of the factory and they bought ice cream and left donations, because like everybody else they wanted to help. Everybody who heard the tale was moved by the story of a village that was trying to save itself. People were always touched when they heard about Moutsouna; some of them laughed with joy, some cheered or clapped, and some, who had quite forgotten what it meant for people to do things together, and help one another, why those people even had tears in their eyes.

The time of doing without did not last so very long, but it was a time that everybody in Moutsouna remembered and talked about for many years after, for even though people did without they were rich in many other ways. There was always plenty of talk and laughter, plenty of good sharing and fun.

The ice-cream factory grew in strength until a day came when Papa Papadopolos, who had been elected by popular demand to manage the factory, was able to give all the workers a proper wage. The villagers set the factory up as a workers' co-operative, which meant everyone in the village owned it and helped make decisions about how it was run. It meant that whenever anything new occurred, like the purchase of a refrigerated lorry to deliver ice cream across the island, or the invention of a new flavour or new ice lolly shape, all the people of Moutsouna, the mothers and the fathers, the grandparents and children and babies, all turned out to pass comments and offer advice and make decisions.

Moutsouna Ice Cream came to be exported to all the other islands in the Aegean. Before long it was being sold in shops right across the mainland of Greece. It was even sold in Athens. In time every one in Greece had heard the story of Moutsouna Ice Cream, but this was not because Moutsouna Ice Cream was available in every shop in the country, it was because Nina finally sat down and finished her book. It was, of course, this book that you are reading now and it was the kind of story that people liked because it was about children and ice cream, and it was a popular story because it reminded readers that when people work together anything is possible.

It was not an easy book for Nina to write because so much had happened and so many people had done so many things to help with the ice dream. At first Nina tried to write down all the things that people had done, but she found herself filling up notebook after notebook with details of village babies who had cut their first teeth, or taken their first steps during the excitement. She wrote about the time Ios' mother cut her finger slicing a lemon, and about a cockerel that caught a cold and couldn't crow properly, and about many other small incidents, until she realised her book would never be finished if she carried on that way. Her grandfather advised her that some of the villagers were private people who might not want to be made famous by being in a book, and so Nina decided she would only

really write about the people in her own family, which was what she had wanted to do right from the start.

In the end Nina was glad not to have written too much about other people in her book, because after it was published visitors came to Moutsouna more than ever. And once the visitors had walked around the harbour and strolled along the beach noticing all the changes and developments that had happened to the sleepy, little village of Nina's story, they began to look at all the villagers themselves. They wanted to know who was who and what they had done to help the ice dream come to life.

For the most part visitors could not tell who people were unless they went right up to them and asked, yet there was always one character they recognised when they reached Moutsouna. In fact many visitors recognised him in Apiranthos and even in Naxos Town because, despite all the small changes in the village, one thing remained the same: on Mondays, Wednesdays and Fridays, Filipos

Velcanos still drove the bus. It didn't seem to matter how many years went by, he still drove it in exactly the same way. He still welcomed everything with a smile. He was glad for the dangerous road, unafraid that it had no wall to protect you. He was glad for the stray goats and the dropped melons. He welcomed the tired, old grandfathers that shuffled aboard slowly and he made time for the small children who ran and tripped and dropped their Moutsouna Ice Creams. He had a smile for everything and everyone, driving with his heart in his hand, ever ready to hand it out whenever it was needed.

Mama says: It was the Chinese who first taught the Arabic people the art of making iced desserts and drinks. They saved winter snow in caves and specially built icehouses, so that they could have ice cream in summer. It was Marco Polo who brought the invention to Europe in the 13th century. To make really smooth ice cream the mixture has to be kept moving while it freezes so ice crystals can't form and make the mixture sharp on the tongue. Modern, electric ice-cream makers do this and take away all the hard turning work that Alex and Nina had to do. Such machines can be fun things to own, but you don't need one to make the following recipes.

Mama's Vanilla Ice Cream

> 500 ml cream
> 4 egg yolks
> 3-4 drops vanilla essence
> 2 teaspoons custard powder
> 1 heaped tablespoon caster sugar

1 Whip half the cream (250ml) until it thickens. Chill in the fridge with an empty plastic box & lid.

2 Make the custard. Separate the egg yolks from the whites in a medium-sized bowl.

3 Beat the yolks, vanilla essence, sugar and custard powder together until the mixture is smooth.

4 Heat the remaining cream (250 ml) until nearly boiling. Do not let it boil.

5 Whisk the hot cream into the yolk mixture.

6 Pour the mixture into the saucepan and whisk over a medium heat until it thickens and comes back up to boiling.

7 Pour the custard into a bowl. Place the bowl of custard into a bowl of cold water. Stir it every once in while.

8 When the custard is cold, fold in the whipped cream. Pour the whole lot into the cold plastic box and freeze.

9 After two hours scoop the ice cream into a large bowl and whisk again. This will help break up any ice-crystals. Put the ice cream back in the freezer until it is refrozen. Then enjoy!

Easy Ice Lollies

You will need:

> * Pots & sticks or you can buy special plastic lolly moulds from kitchen shops
> * Real fruit juice or yogurt

Pour the fruit juice into the pots and add the sticks. Put them in the freezer until solid. You can experiment by adding chunks of real fruit, chocolate sprinkles or other treats or you can try lining the moulds with melted chocolate, freezing them and then pouring the juice in on top.